W9-DGO-818

Where No Sun Shines

LEO P. KELLEY

CHILDRENS PRESS, CHICAGO

The Galaxy 5 Series

Good-bye to Earth
On the Red World
Vacation in Space
Dead Moon
Where No Sun Shines
King of the Stars

Childrens Press Edition

Series Director: Robert G. Bander
Designer: Richard Kharibian
Cover and illustrations: Rick Guidice

ISBN-0-516-02256-3

Library of Congress Catalog Card Number: 78-68229

Printed in the United States of America.

1. 9 8 7 6 5 4 3 2

CONTENTS

CHAPTER 1

A SHIP IN TROUBLE

The spaceship had a name painted on its side:

CAPTAIN KANE'S SPACE STORE

Under the name were more words:

WE BUY AND SELL EVERYTHING

It was a small ship and it wasn't in very good shape. In fact, it was in trouble. One of its three jets had stopped firing some time ago. Now another one was about to do the same.

The captain on board the ship shouted orders to his two crew members.

"Get that jet firing again! We don't want to spend the rest of our lives floating out here with the stars!"

His crew members—one was a human, the other was an alien—did the best they could. The alien had blue skin and four arms. His name was Tufo. Tufo pressed buttons on the ship's control board. Carl, the human crew member, rolled up his dirty shirt sleeves. He turned a big red dial. But the dial wouldn't work. Its face read: 000000.

"It's no use, Captain Kane," said Tufo. "We're losing our second jet."

Carl turned the dial again. But nothing happened. He said, "It looks like we're done for, Captain Kane. The jet just won't hold up. It's going out on us."

Captain Kane pushed his two crew members out of his way. He sat down in front of the control board.

"You're so dumb—you couldn't be right!" he shouted at his crew. He turned dials and pressed buttons.

He was a tall, thin man and no longer young. His eyes were black, his hair was white, and his face was very red.

"I never should have bought a secondhand

ship!" he shouted. "But a new one costs too much. And I'm a poor man. Never trust a secondhand spaceship dealer."

The second jet went dead.

Captain Kane, angry, smashed his hand against the control board. He broke the jet-firing machine.

"Send out a call for help!" he ordered. "Are there any other ships near us? *Answer me, someone!"*

The alien went to the control board.

"Where do you think you're going?" Captain Kane asked him.

"You said to send out a distress call, Captain," Tufo said.

"I did? Oh, yes, I did, didn't I? Well, don't just stand there. *Send* the distress call." He stood up.

Tufo sat down at the control board and sent the distress call. No answer.

"Send it again!" Captain Kane shouted, looking as if he were about to blow up. "Isn't there anyone out there who will come to help an old man?"

Finally, the ship's distress call got an answer. A woman's voice came over the ship's radio. "This is Ellen Drake on the spaceship Voyager. We got your distress call. Please tell us where you are. We'll come at once."

"Get out of my way!" shouted Captain Kane. He pushed Tufo away from the control board.

Then, in a sweet voice, he said, "We read you, Voyager. Thank you for answering our call. I'm a poor man, but you can be sure I'll pay you for your help."

"We don't want any pay," Ellen said. "Tell us where you are."

"Yes, yes," said Captain Kane. "Of course. I'm not quite sure *where* we are, as a matter of fact. Can you hold on for a minute?"

To Carl he said, "Where are we?"

The man checked his star maps and told Captain Kane where they were in space. Captain Kane then told Ellen Drake.

She said, "We'll be there in 20 minutes. Over and out."

Captain Kane went to a window of his ship and looked out. "Stars," he said. "That's all you see out here in space. Stars and still more stars. I'm so sick of looking at stars. I should close my space store for good. I should go back to Earth. Buy a little house. Plant a little garden. Take it easy for the few years that are left to me."

"Captain Kane," said Tufo. "Our third jet is about to give out."

"*Everything* is against me!" shouted Captain Kane. "Everything *has* been since I was a child. It's just not *fair*!" He put his hands to his head. Then he looked up. "If I get out of here in one piece, I'm going to find the man who sold me this ship. I'm going to make *him* fly it!"

The last jet died.

Captain Kane's ship, not able to move without its jets, floated in space. On board, Captain Kane and his crew could only sit and wait for the spaceship Voyager to find them.

CHAPTER 2

HELP ON ITS WAY

On the spaceship Voyager, Ellen Drake sat by herself in the ship's control room. She pressed several buttons on the control board in front of her. When colored lights flashed on the board, she made some notes on a piece of paper.

Then she checked her star maps with care. When she had finished, she made more notes.

She had found that Voyager was in good shape and right on course. It would be a long time yet before the ship reached Planet 1 of Star 84 in Galaxy 5.

Ellen pressed another button. She turned

to the great window screens. As she did so, Steve Estrada came into the control room. He saw a yellow light flash on the control board and came to a stop. He looked at Ellen.

"What's wrong?" he asked her. "Why are we going off course?"

"Hello, Estrada," Ellen said. "I didn't hear you come in. To answer your question, I just changed Voyager's course."

"Why?"

"A little while ago I got a distress call from another spaceship. The ship's in trouble. I told the man who spoke to me that we would come to where he is and try to help him."

"Who did you speak to? What's the name of the ship? What's wrong with it?"

"I don't know."

"But you're supposed to ask those questions when you pick up a call for help."

"I know I should have asked. But I really didn't think it was all that important. After all, the ship's in trouble. What more did I really need to know?"

Don Chadrow came into the control room. "What's this about trouble? Who's in trouble?"

Ellen told Don what she had just told Steve. When she had finished, he said, "I hope we'll be able to help out when we reach the ship."

Steve said, "I'd feel a whole lot better if I knew more about the ship and who's on it."

"What does that matter?" Don asked him. "The important thing is that we go and try to help the ship."

"That's what I told Estrada," Ellen said. "But he has other ideas."

"There are good ships and bad ships in space," Steve said. "Just as there are good and bad people in space. We've already learned this the hard way. That's why I think you should have found out more about the ship before we go to it."

"Well," Ellen said, "I suppose you're right. Do you want me to get in touch with the ship again and find out all about it?"

For a few seconds, Steve didn't say anything. Then, "No, I guess everything will be OK."

"Sure it will be," said Don. "Don't worry so much about everything, Estrada. Your trouble is that you always have to do everything by the book. By the rules."

"That's my way of looking at things, as you know," Steve said. "I believe in following rules. That way you stay out of trouble."

"And maybe miss the fun," Don said with a smile.

Steve didn't say anything more. He helped Ellen at the control board.

It wasn't long before Captain Kane's ship came into sight through the great windows.

"That's the ship," Ellen said. "It's right where the man told me it would be."

"It sure doesn't look like much of a ship to me," Steve said. "It looks pretty far gone."

"That's our job," Ellen said. "To try to put the pieces back together."

She got in touch with the ship. She spoke to Captain Kane. "Please be sure your docking machine is in order. We'll begin our docking moves as soon as you're ready. Over."

Strange noises could be heard coming from Captain Kane's ship. Once in a while, a voice could be heard shouting.

Then Captain Kane spoke to Ellen from his ship. "I'm really so very sorry to keep you waiting like this. But it seems that our docking machine isn't in the very best of shape. My crew is trying to get it in order. Please stand by."

Five minutes passed. Then Captain Kane told Ellen that Voyager could dock with his ship. Everything was now fine with his ship's docking machine, he said.

But that turned out not to be true. As Voyager began to dock with Captain Kane's ship, there was trouble. The two ships couldn't dock at first. But finally the docking was completed.

"We made it," Don said as he watched the docking on the video screen. "For a few minutes there, I thought we'd had it."

"Me too," Ellen said. "Let's board the other ship and see what we can do to help out."

With Steve and Don at her side, she went

to Voyager's air lock. Once through it, they came into the air lock of the other ship. Captain Kane opened it for them, and they came out into his ship.

"I'm Ellen Drake," Ellen said to Captain Kane. She held out her hand to him.

"Oh, I'm so very glad to see you, Ellen," Captain Kane said. He bent over and kissed her hand. "I do hope you can help us."

"This is Steve Estrada," Ellen said.

Captain Kane shook hands with Steve.

"And this is Don Chadrow," she told Captain Kane.

Don stepped forward and shook hands with Captain Kane.

"What's wrong with your ship?" Steve asked.

"Everything," answered Captain Kane. "Well, not really everything. It's our jets. All three of them are as dead as burned-out suns. We don't know what's wrong with them. And we haven't been able to fix them."

"We'll see what we can do about them," Steve said. "Come on, Drake. You too, Chadrow."

The three of them left the room. Soon they could be heard working on the ship's jets.

Captain Kane walked around the room.

Then he went into the air lock and came out on the spaceship Voyager. He went from place to place on the ship. He came into a room that held many glass boxes. Inside each box was a man or woman.

"What's this?" he said out loud. Then he began to count the boxes. He soon gave up counting. There were just too many boxes. He stood there looking at them and thinking.

It had been a long time since he had seen so many humans in this part of space. And, thinking about that fact, he had an idea. For the first time in a long time, he felt happy. He rushed back to his own ship.

Some time later, Steve, Ellen, and Don found him in his control room. There was a big smile on his face.

"Your jets are fixed," Steve told him. "You can turn them on now."

"Turn them on," Captain Kane ordered the four-armed Tufo.

"Sorry, Captain," said Tufo. "I can't. The control board is broken."

"Broken? Who broke it?"

"You did, Captain," Carl said.

"Oh," said Captain Kane. "I forgot. Well, I couldn't help it. But now. . . ."

"Let me take a look at it," Ellen said. She did. "Your jet-firing machine is broken. But it won't be too hard to fix. Give me a few minutes."

She used her tools. Then she told Captain Kane that the jet-firing machine was fixed.

"Good luck to you," Steve said to Captain Kane. He turned to leave the ship.

So did Ellen and Don.

"Wait!" said Captain Kane. "I should pay you for helping me."

"Forget it," Don said. "We were glad to help you."

"Wait!" Captain Kane said again. "While you were fixing my ship, I just happened to go on board yours. I do hope you don't mind?"

"Not at all," Ellen said.

"Good. You have a beautiful ship. Yes, beautiful. Not like this death trap of mine. While I was on your ship, I saw some people in big glass boxes. They're not dead, are they?"

Ellen shook her head. She explained that the people were in a deep sleep. They would sleep until Voyager reached Planet 1 of Star 84 in Galaxy 5, she said. When the ship got there, the people would wake up. Then they would all build an Earth Colony on Planet 1.

"If they woke up now, or if they were made to wake up. . . ." Captain Kane seemed to be thinking out loud.

"They would die," Steve told him.

"Oh, that's too bad," Captain Kane said. "I had thought—well, never mind."

"Good-bye," Ellen said. Then she, Don, and Steve left the ship.

When they were gone, Captain Kane spoke to his two crew members.

"The aliens in this part of space have never seen a human being other than me. And you, of course," he added, pointing to Carl. "Am I right?"

"Yes, Captain," said Carl, "you're right."

"What are you getting at, Captain?" asked Tufo.

Captain Kane told them.

Carl began to smile. So did Tufo.

"Get your guns," Captain Kane said. "We're going on board Voyager."

CHAPTER 3

CAPTAIN KANE'S PLAN

"What a funny man he was," Ellen said. She stood in front of Voyager's control board. "But he was nice to us."

"I'm not so sure his head is in the right place," Don said.

"Well, he *did* lower it to kiss my hand," Ellen laughed. She turned a dial.

"That was really too much. No one kisses hands in the 21st century!" Steve said, and smiled at Don.

"Maybe we'll have to do something about that," Don said.

"Maybe," said Steve, winking at Ellen.

Ellen had stopped laughing. She looked out the window screen and read the words painted on the side of Captain Kane's ship.

"I wonder what he buys and sells?" she said.

Just then, Captain Kane, Carl, and Tufo came through the air lock into Voyager.

"Anything and everything is the answer to your question," Captain Kane said. "You'd be surprised at some of the things I sell. I mean you *will* be surprised."

Steve turned from the window screen. Ellen looked up from the control board. Don put down the book he had been reading. All of them were too surprised to speak at first.

Six guns pointed at them. Captain Kane and Carl each had one. Tufo had four—one in each of his four-fingered hands.

"What are you doing here?" Ellen asked.

"Put those guns away," Steve said.

Don didn't say a thing. He kept his eyes on Captain Kane.

"Please don't any of you move—not even a little bit," Captain Kane said. "If you move, you're dead. And I don't want any of you to die. Please believe me about that."

Don moved closer to Steve, but he still didn't say anything.

"I told you not to move!" Captain Kane shouted at him.

Don stood still.

"That's better, much better." Captain Kane gave an order to his two crew members. They stepped forward.

"Get on board our ship," Carl said.

Tufo said, "You heard him. *Move!*"

When Ellen and the others didn't move, Tufo looked at Captain Kane. "Shall I shoot them?"

"No!" Captain Kane shouted. "Kick them. Hit them. Knock them down. But don't shoot them. I can't sell dead merchandise."

Captain Kane's words were all that Don needed to hear. Sure now that he would not be shot, he grabbed Tufo from behind. He held on to him. Ellen picked up the book Don had been reading. She threw it across the room. It knocked the gun from Captain Kane's hand.

Steve raced across the room. Carl fired a shot at him. The shot missed. Steve tried to get the gun that Captain Kane had dropped. But Captain Kane got it first. He picked it up and pointed it at Steve. Steve stood still. Then he put his hands up in the air.

At the same time, Tufo threw two of his guns to Carl, who caught them. Then Tufo broke free of Don. He grabbed Ellen with one hand, Don with another. Ellen let out a cry of pain. Tufo's hands were as strong as iron.

"Take them on board our ship," Captain Kane ordered.

Carl forced Steve into the air lock. Behind him came Tufo, who still held Ellen and Don.

Before Tufo got to the lock, Ellen bent down. She bit his hand. He let out a cry and let go of her arm. In a flash, she was across the control room. She got to the control board. Then she seemed to become weak. She fell over the control board. She made soft sounds that might have been words.

Captain Kane crossed the room and made her get up. "Come, now," he said. "No more tricks, if you value your health."

Ellen looked up at him. He smiled. She looked down at the gun in his hand. Then she went to the air lock. She walked through it with Captain Kane right behind her.

Once on the other ship, Captain Kane gave orders to his crew members. Carl left the room. When he returned, he had a key in his hand.

He and Tufo forced Ellen, Don, and Steve down into the bottom of the ship. The big room at the bottom of the ship was filled with many things. Pictures. Clothes. Chairs and tables.

But the clothes were not made for humans to wear. The dresses had spaces for more than two arms. The coats had spaces for several heads. The chairs and tables couldn't be used by humans. They were the wrong sizes and shapes.

There were also several big cages in the room. One cage had a strange animal in it. The animal had a long nose and eyes as big as pies.

Tufo forced Ellen, Steve, and Don to get into the empty cage next to the one with the animal. The animal tried to get at them. It screamed at them. But it couldn't reach them. Tufo shut the door of the cage and locked it.

Captain Kane came into the room.

"What do you plan to do with us?" Steve asked him.

"I could tell you, of course," Captain Kane said with a big smile. "But I think I'd better not. I'm sure you wouldn't like to hear the answer."

"I know the answer," Don said.

"Oh?" said Captain Kane. "You do?"

"You said something before that I found interesting," Don said. "You said you couldn't sell dead merchandise."

"I get it now," Ellen said. "He plans to sell us to someone."

"I'm really sorry you guessed," Captain Kane said. "I'd hoped it would be a surprise.

Not a nice surprise, perhaps, but still a surprise. I've always loved surprises. I thought you would too. Well, now you know."

"Who are you going to sell us to?" Steve asked.

Captain Kane answered, "To the aliens who live on the planet named Zandar. I'd hoped to be able to sell the people in the glass boxes, too. But since you told me they would die if they woke up. . . ."

"What about our ship?" Steve asked. "What are you going to do with Voyager?"

"Why, keep it, of course," answered Captain Kane. "Yours is a much better ship than mine. I'll sell mine if I can find someone dumb enough to buy it from me. After I sell *you*, that is. I'm sure the Zandarians will want to buy you from me. The Zandarians love all kinds of animals."

"But we're not . . . !" Steve began.

"Yes, we are," Don said. "We're animals. Humans don't think of themselves as animals. But that's just what we are."

"What are you, a space pirate?" Ellen asked Kane. "The Space Police will zero in on you."

"Out here?" said Captain Kane. "No way—not in this part of space. There won't be Space

Police until more humans come this far. Then they'll start making all kinds of laws. A man like me will be out of business in no time flat. That will be a sad day for me, a very sad day."

Captain Kane looked as if he were about to cry. But he didn't. His smile returned.

"I think I can get a good price for you," he said. "I think. . . ."

"Captain," whispered Tufo.

"I've told you not to talk when *I'm* talking!"

Tufo whispered again to Captain Kane. "The woman can have children. If we keep her and the two men for a time, we'll have lots of humans to sell. Not just three."

"You son of an alien!" shouted Captain Kane. "Humans aren't like you. You can have children in a few *weeks*. It takes almost a year for a human woman to have a child."

Tufo didn't give up. "You should tell the Zandarians that the woman can have children. They can have many humans because of her—in time, as you say. When the Zandarians know that, they will pay more for these humans."

Ellen turned away.

Steve asked, "What are the Zandarians like?"

"You'll see," said Captain Kane. "But for now I'll tell you just one thing about them. They live in a place where no sun shines."

He left the room. Tufo and Carl followed him out.

Ellen felt the bars of the cage. Strong. She looked at Don and Steve.

"We're trapped," Don said. "And to think that we helped him fix his ship. Just a funny old hand-kisser."

Ellen began to laugh. "If I hadn't answered his call for help. . . ."

Her laughter was too loud. Too sharp.

"Take it easy, Drake," Steve told her. He shook her.

She stopped laughing.

CHAPTER 4

CAGED

Ellen sat on the floor of the cage where she had been put by Captain Kane. She looked down at the floor. But she really didn't see it. She was lost in her thoughts.

Her thoughts were not happy ones. She thought about the time Captain Kane had sent his call for help. That was the beginning. Now she was here. Where would she end up? she wondered.

She thought she would give anything to be back on board Voyager and on her way with Steve and Don to Galaxy 5. But she was here.

In this cage. And it was all her own fault.

She looked across at Steve. He had been right, she thought. He had told her she should have asked for facts about who was sending the call for help. It could have been a trick. She had heard of that kind of thing happening in space. And yet she had asked Kane no questions–not even his name. She had just said that she would come. Being too trusting had caused her problems on Earth, too. So she had said good-bye to John–and good-bye to Earth.

And now she had got herself in trouble again. But that was not the worst thing. She had got Steve and Don in trouble, too. And now there was no way to say good-bye to that.

Steve saw that she was looking at him. He crossed to where she was sitting. "I know what you're thinking," he said, as he sat down beside her.

"Do you?"

"Don't think that this is all your fault."

"That isn't exactly what I was thinking."

Steve shook his head. "Yes, it was. You did make a mistake by not asking Kane who he was and other questions. But you only wanted to help a person in trouble. *I* should have asked Kane a few questions myself when we first went on board his ship. I should have kept my eyes open and not let him take us by surprise the way he did later on."

Ellen said, "Thanks for trying to make me feel better."

"Your feelings are your own business," Steve said. "But I'm telling you that the spot we're in now is as much my fault as it is yours. From now on, both of us are going to have to be more careful."

"Do you think we could break out of here?" Ellen asked.

Instead of answering her, Steve got up and took hold of the bars of the cage. He tried to shake them. They didn't move at all. Then he tried to open the lock on the door of the cage. He had no luck.

He returned to Ellen. "We're just going to have to wait to see what Kane and his crew do next. Maybe we can think how to get away once they let us out of here."

Steve and Ellen stopped talking. Both of them became lost in their own thoughts.

Don got up from where he had been sitting and began to walk around the cage. Like Steve, he tried to open the lock on the cage's door. When he couldn't, he gave it a kick. But the door stayed locked. He kept on walking as if he had to do something—anything.

Like Steve and Ellen, Don seemed to be lost in thought. He wasn't really watching where he was going or what was around him. As he was walking he moved too close to the bars on one side of the cage. On the other side of the bars was the wild animal in its own cage. It had been sleeping. But as Don passed by, it woke up. It reached through the bars and grabbed him.

Don let out a cry.

The animal held him in both of its front

paws. It tried to pull him through the bars of its cage. Ellen and Steve jumped to their feet and ran to Don. Both of them tried to pull him free. But the animal wouldn't let go of Don. It held on to him as he tried to set himself free.

"Hit it with something!" Ellen said. She looked around the cage. But there was nothing in it that she could use to hit the animal.

Steve hit the animal's paws with his hands. But still it wouldn't let go of Don.

Then Ellen did the only thing she could think of to do. She bit one of the animal's paws as hard as she could. The animal screamed and let go of Don, who ran to the far side of the cage. Then the angry animal tried to grab Ellen. But she jumped back out of its reach just in time.

"Are you OK, Chadrow?" she asked.

"I think so," he answered. "But that animal was ready to eat me for dinner. It would have if it hadn't been for you."

"We'd all better stay over here on this side of the cage," Steve said. "We don't want any more trouble with that animal. It's another Captain Kane."

The three of them sat down. Thinking. Waiting. For what?

CHAPTER 5

WHERE NO SUN SHINES

Suddenly, there was the sound of shouting on the ship.

"That's Captain Kane," Steve said. "I wonder what. . . ."

Captain Kane stormed down to the bottom of his ship. "I can't fly Voyager!" he shouted. "I can't make it work at all. The controls are locked. What did you do to your ship?"

"I don't know what you're talking about," Steve told him.

"I don't either," Don said.

Ellen said nothing. She just smiled.

Captain Kane looked at her. "Why are you smiling?"

Ellen stopped smiling.

Captain Kane came close to the cage. "Do you want to tell me something, child?"

Ellen didn't speak.

Captain Kane studied her face. "I remember now," he said. "When you got away from us before. . . . You ran to the control board and fell over it. You did something to the ship's controls, didn't you? That's why I can't fly Voyager."

When Ellen didn't answer, Captain Kane ordered Tufo to take her out of the cage. Carl unlocked the cage.

Tufo went into it and grabbed Ellen. Steve and Don tried to fight the alien, but he pushed them both back. They fell and hit the bars at the back of the cage. Tufo pulled Ellen from the cage.

"Now then," said Captain Kane, "let's board Voyager."

When they were in Voyager's control room, Captain Kane spoke. "Fix this ship so I can fly it."

Ellen made no move. She wouldn't even look at Captain Kane. He spoke to Carl, who put his hands around Ellen's neck. Ellen tried to pull his hands away. But Tufo stopped her.

She couldn't speak or catch her breath. She suddenly felt weak. The control room began to spin before her eyes. She heard Captain Kane speaking to her. His voice seemed to come from far away.

"Fix this ship," he said, "or die. I'll be sorry to see you die. That will leave only your two friends to sell. But I would have no choice."

Carl took his hands from Ellen's neck. She rubbed her neck as her eyes cleared.

"Well?" said Captain Kane.

"You're right," Ellen said to him in a low voice. "I told Voyager to lock the ship's controls."

"You mean Voyager can *hear* you?"

"Yes. And the ship can speak, too."

"How wonderful!" said Captain Kane. I think I'm going to enjoy flying this ship. Fix it now."

"Voyager," Ellen said, "unlock the controls."

"I SHALL DO SO AT ONCE," Voyager said.

"Did you hear that?" Captain Kane said to his crew. "A talking spaceship!"

He went to the control board. He pressed

a button, turned a dial. Nothing happened.

"What's wrong *now?*" he shouted. He kept trying to fly the ship, but he couldn't. "This ship has more buttons and dials than any I've ever seen," he said. "I just don't know how to make it fly."

He turned back to Ellen. "But *you* do, don't you, child?"

Ellen looked down at the floor.

"Would you like *my* hands around your neck this time?" Captain Kane asked her.

Ellen decided to follow Kane's orders for the moment. She went to the control board. "Voyager is ready to fly now. But I don't know where Zandar is."

"I do," said Captain Kane. "So I'll stay here with you on Voyager." He sent Carl and Tufo back to the other ship. He told them to follow behind Voyager. He waited until his ship left the side of Voyager. Then he told Ellen how to find the planet Zandar.

Voyager flew off into space with Ellen at the ship's controls. Beside her stood Captain Kane, a gun in his hand. Behind Voyager came Captain Kane's ship.

Both ships flew through space for a long time

before they reached Zandar. Ellen brought the ship down on the planet. Minutes later, the other ship also landed.

"Come with me," Captain Kane said to Ellen. He forced her to leave Voyager and board his ship.

Once there, he turned her over to the alien. Tufo took her to the bottom of the ship. He put her back in the cage with Steve and Don. Then he left.

"Are you OK?" Don asked her. "They didn't hurt you, did they?"

Ellen told them what had happened.

"So now we're on Zandar," Steve said.

"There's something funny about all this," Ellen said. "Do you remember that Captain Kane said we were going to a place where no sun shines?"

"Yes, I remember that," Steve said. "So what's funny?"

"This planet *has* a sun," Ellen told him. "I saw it as we landed."

"Then maybe this isn't Zandar after all," Don said.

"Captain Kane said it was," Ellen said.

"We'll just have to wait to find out," Steve said.

They had a long time to wait. But finally Tufo returned. He was carrying chains. Each chain had a collar on one end. Minutes later, Carl joined Tufo.

One by one, they took Ellen, Don, and Steve from the cage. Each of the prisoners struggled, but Kane's men held them fast and put collars around each of their necks. Then Tufo picked up the other ends of the chains and made them walk behind him.

Tufo led them from the ship. Carl went with them, his gun in his hand. Once outside the ship, Ellen, Don, and Steve found themselves bouncing along the ground. Carl and Tufo also bounced along.

"Zandar must have a very low gravity," Steve said. "That's why we feel so light and can bounce like this."

Tufo led them on, holding on to their chains.

As they moved on, they looked for the Zandarians but saw no one.

Soon they came to a big door set in the ground. Tufo and Carl opened the door, and everyone climbed down steps that went down into the ground. Along the way, fires burned in holes in the walls, but the flames didn't give off much light.

Some time later, the prisoners came to the bottom of the steps. And into a city—a city under the ground.

"Those houses!" Steve whispered to Ellen. "They're the biggest houses I've ever seen. They must be ten times bigger than houses on Earth."

"What's that round thing over there?" Ellen asked him. "Is *that* some kind of house?"

Ellen pointed to a large red ball that sat in front of one of the houses.

"I don't know what it is," Steve said. "Do you, Chadrow?"

Don shook his head. Then a door opened in the house. The top of the door was more than

40 feet from the ground. In the door stood Captain Kane.

"How could he open a door that big?" Ellen asked.

"*He* didn't," Don said. "*That's* who did. *Look!*"

A Zandarian stood in the door. Its head looked almost human, but it had no hair. Its skin was the color of smoke. It had two arms and two legs. It wore a long green dress that covered most of its body.

"Just look at that Zandarian!" Don said. "It's a real giant. It's four times as tall as Captain Kane, and *he's* about six feet tall!"

The Zandarian bent down, picked up the red ball, and began to bounce it. Captain Kane shouted up at the Zandarian.

"What's he saying?" Don asked.

Steve shook his head. "I don't know. He must be speaking Zandarian."

Ellen said, "I don't know what he said either, but I don't like the way that Zandarian is looking at us."

CHAPTER 6

SOLD TO THE ZANDARIANS

The Zandarian dropped the ball and went back inside the house.

Captain Kane bounced over to Ellen and the others. "That," he said, "was a Zandarian."

"We didn't think it was King Kong," Don said.

"Very funny," said Captain Kane. "As a matter of fact, it couldn't have been King Kong. Because you see, it was a girl. Just a child."

Tufo laughed. So did Carl. But Ellen didn't. Steve and Don didn't either.

Then Steve asked a question. "Why do the Zandarians live down here?"

"Because the sun burns their skin," said Captain Kane. "They can't stand the sun. So they dug down into the ground to build their city here. If they stayed in the sun too long, it would kill them."

"A child," Ellen said as if she were talking to herself. "I wonder how tall the Zandarians grow?"

"There's your answer," said Captain Kane. He pointed to the door of the house. "Here comes the girl with her mother."

"I don't believe it," Steve said. "And yet I'm seeing it. That girl's mother must be almost 40 feet tall."

The mother and child came up to them. The girl bent down and reached for Ellen. Her mother spoke some Zandarian words and pulled the child's hand away from Ellen. The child said something in Zandarian. Her voice and the voice of her mother sounded like thunder.

"What are they saying?" Steve asked Captain Kane.

"The child likes you," Captain Kane answered. "She thinks you'll make nice pets. The girl wants her mother to buy all of you. Her mother says the child can have only one of you. But I'll see to it that the girl gets what she wants—all three of you."

He spoke to the Zandarian mother. The mother shook her head, and the girl began to cry. Captain Kane went on talking to her mother.

Finally, the mother took a bright jewel from a pocket in her dress. She showed it to Captain Kane. He shook his head.

The girl pulled at her mother's dress. The mother put the jewel back in her pocket and took out a bigger one.

"That's better, but still not good enough," Captain Kane said to his crew members. Then he shouted up at the Zandarian mother.

Finally, she took out a very big jewel. It kept changing colors. First it was yellow, then blue, then red.

Captain Kane smiled at the Zandarian. He told Tufo to give the chains to the girl. The alien did. The girl took the chains and began to do a little dance. After putting the jewel on the ground, the mother went toward her house.

"You've just been sold," Captain Kane said

to Ellen, Steve, and Don. "I hope you'll enjoy your new life as pets."

He gave orders to his crew. The three of them tried to lift the big, bright jewel. But it was too big—bigger than they were. So they began to roll it toward the steps that led to the ground above.

The girl stopped her dance. She began to run after her mother, holding the ends of the chains in her hand. Ellen was the first to fall down. Then Steve and Don fell too. The child ran too fast for them. They couldn't keep up with her. The child pulled them along the ground behind her.

But then the girl's mother looked back and saw what was happening. She stopped her daughter and spoke to her. The child bent down to help her new pets get to their feet. Then she began to play with them as her mother went inside the house.

As the girl picked her up, Ellen let out a wild cry. Pain flew through her body. The child was holding her too tight. She thought her bones were going to break.

"Hold on to the kid's fingers!" Steve shouted up to her. "Don't let go!"

Ellen did as she had been told. Down below

her—far below—was the ground. She closed her eyes as she thought, What if this child drops me?

The girl gave a happy laugh that filled the air with more thunder. Then she put Ellen down and picked up Steve. She took hold of the long chain fastened to his neck. Then she began to swing him in a circle around her head.

Steve couldn't get his breath. The tight collar was choking him as he went around and around in the air. He waved his hands, tried to speak, but couldn't. The child kept swinging him in a circle.

Suddenly, everything went black.

Ellen and Don screamed at the child. Just then her mother came out of the house. She spoke sharp Zandarian words. The child put Steve down. He lay on the ground and didn't move. The child touched him with one finger. She rolled him over. Still he didn't move.

Again the mother spoke to the child. First she took the collar off Steve's neck. Then she took the collars off Ellen and Don, too.

"Now!" Don shouted to Ellen. "Let's get out of here!"

They both picked up Steve. Then they began to bounce along the ground toward the steps

that led above the ground. The child laughed as she watched them.

"We're going to make it!" Don shouted. "The steps aren't far away now."

They had almost reached them when the child took two steps. Then she bent down and picked up Ellen, Don, and Steve in one hand.

Her mother spoke to her. The child carried her three pets into the house. Then she put them in a big box and went away.

Ellen, out of breath, couldn't speak for a minute. Don couldn't either. Both of them bent over Steve. Ellen rubbed his hands and face. At last, he opened his eyes. He put his hands around his neck.

"I thought that kid was going to kill me," he said.

"How do you feel?" Ellen asked him. There was a worried look on her face as she watched him.

"Bad."

Ellen looked away from him and up at the top of the box that was so high above her head. "There's one thing for sure," she said.

"What's that?" Don asked her.

Still looking up at the top of the box, Ellen answered, "We've just got to get out of here."

"True," Don said. He too looked up at the top of the box. "But the question is—*how* do we get out of here? We can't reach the top of this box. Even if you stood on my shoulders, Ellen, you still couldn't reach the top of the box."

"You're right," she said. Then she didn't say anything for several minutes while she thought about their problem.

Suddenly, her face brightened. "I think we just might be able to get to the top of that box," she said.

"How?" Steve asked her.

"Zandar has a very low gravity," Ellen said and smiled at the two men who were watching her.

"I get it!" Steve said. "I'd forgotten about Zandar's low gravity. I think we *can* get to the top of this box without too much trouble."

"You've lost me," Don said. "What's this about Zandar's low gravity? What's the planet's low gravity got to do with us and this box that kid put us in?"

Ellen explained. "If Zandar had gravity like we have on Earth, the Zandarians wouldn't be able to move at all because they're so big. But because the gravity is low here on Zandar, *we're* able to move easily. We don't weigh as much here on Zandar as we do on Earth. So maybe we could jump high enough to get to the top of the box and then get out."

"Got you," Don said. "Do you want to give it a try, Ellen?"

Ellen laughed. "Sure."

Don and Steve both moved to one side of the box to give Ellen room to jump.

"I'm not sure how hard I'll have to jump so that I can reach the top," Ellen said.

"Just be careful," Steve said. "If you jump too high, you might go right over the top. You'll have to jump just high enough so you can catch it."

"Take it easy on the first jump," Don told Ellen.

"OK," Ellen said. "I'll give it a try."

She did. The first time she jumped, she didn't get even half way up the side of the box. The second time she jumped, she got almost to the top of the box. Then she tried a third time.

"You made it!" Steve yelled. "Good for you! Hang on!"

Ellen had reached the top of the box and grabbed it with both of her hands. She held on to it as tight as she could.

Little by little, she pulled herself up and then was able to sit on top of the box. She threw a leg over the side of the box and then looked down at Steve and Don.

"I sure am glad Zandar is a low-gravity planet," she said. "If it weren't, we might have had to spend the rest of our lives as Zandarian pets."

"We're not out of this tight spot yet," Steve said. "We've still got a long way to go before we're home free. Drop down outside the box, Ellen. Then Don and I will join you."

Ellen looked down at the floor outside the box. It was a long way down. Could she get down without hurting herself? Suddenly, she felt afraid to try to jump down to the floor.

As if he knew she was afraid, Steve said, "You can make it, Drake. I'm sure you can."

The sound of his voice made Ellen feel better. But she was still a little bit afraid. Jumping up was one thing. But jumping down was different. Still, she knew she couldn't just stay where she was. And she would have to jump down on one side of the box or the other.

She threw her other leg over the top of the box. Then she jumped.

She landed on her feet and then she felt herself going up again. Then she fell to the floor. At first, she didn't move. Had she broken anything?

No. She was OK.

She got up and looked up at the top of the box. Suddenly, Don was there. There was a big smile on his face. He jumped down beside Ellen. Then Steve was on top of the box. He too jumped down to join them.

"So that's that," said Don. "Goodbye, box!" he added. "Now what?"

"Now we've got to find a way out of the giants' house," Steve said, looking around the room.

"There's the door over there," Ellen said, pointing. "But it's so big! We'll never be able to open it."

"Maybe we can," Steve said. He looked around. "Let's get that kid's toy house over there! We can push it up against the door. We can probably reach the door handle from inside the toy house."

The three of them ran to it. They pushed it across the room until it was against the door. Then they went into it and climbed the steps to the top floor. They looked out a window. The handle of the big door was right in front of them.

They tried hard to turn it but it didn't move.

"We could try to break one of the windows of the giants' house," Ellen said.

"With what?" Don asked. "Everything they have is too big for us to lift."

"I don't mean the things that belong to the Zandarians," Ellen said. "I mean we could throw some of the things here in the toy house at the window. We can lift *them*."

She picked up a toy chair. She threw it at the big window. It never reached the window.

Instead, it fell on the giants' table. As it did, it knocked some dishes off the table.

They fell to the floor with a crash.

Hearing the loud noise, the mother came into the room. When she saw what was happening, she picked up the toy house and shook it.

Steve fell out of the house through one of its windows. He picked himself up and began to run. Ellen and Don also fell out of the house through another window. They ran too.

The mother took just two steps. Then she reached down and picked up Steve. She put him back in the box. Then she turned to look for Ellen and Don.

She bent down and reached out her big hand. Don and Ellen ran. But Don didn't get far. The giant caught him and put him in the box with Steve.

When Ellen saw what had happened, she thought she might be able to hide from the giant. But what would be the point? Even if she got away, she couldn't just leave Steve and Don where they were. She stepped out of her hiding place and let the giant pick her up and put her back in the box.

"I've had it," Steve said when they were all together again. "I've had it with being a pet. I can take floating in space, space fever—anything but this."

"We could try once more to get out," Ellen said. "All we have to do is wait until that giant goes away and then. . . ."

Suddenly, the giant's face could be seen

above the box. She put a top on the box. Steve, Ellen, and Don found themselves in darkness.

"That's that," Don said. "We might as well get some sleep. Maybe we can try again when the top is taken off this box."

'If Captain Kane and the others get to Voyager. . . ." Steve stopped talking.

"But he can't fly Voyager," Ellen said. "He needed me to fly the ship before."

"But he saw how you did it, right?"

"Yes, he did, and he may know how to fly Voyager from watching me do it. But remember, Voyager has a mind of its own."

"If Captain Kane can fool us, he can outfox Voyager," Don said. "We've got to get out and stop him or Voyager will be gone forever."

"And we'll be pets forever," Steve said.

CHAPTER 7

FEAR OF FIRE

The three human pets were sleeping when the child returned. But they woke up fast when they felt the child's hands on them.

The girl picked Ellen up in one hand and Steve and Don in the other. She took them from the box, carried them outside to the house next to hers, and knocked on the door. It was opened by a Zandarian boy.

The girl spoke to him and showed him what she had in her hands. When the boy reached for Ellen, the girl pulled her hand back. Then the Zandarian girl and boy went outside to play. The girl put her pets down on the ground.

Steve looked around. "The steps are over that way," he said. "Get ready. I'll tell you when to make a run for it."

The girl picked Steve up and handed him to the boy. The boy shook Steve and said something. Then he shook him again. The girl reached for Steve. The boy put his hands behind his back.

"We've got to do something!" Ellen said. "Those kids will hurt Estrada again!"

Don looked down at the ground. There were sticks and stones here and there that would seem small to the Zandarians. But they were all too big and heavy for Don to lift.

"Our chains!" Ellen said. "Let's get our chains. We can hit the children with them. Maybe we can make them let Estrada go."

"Where are they?" Then Don remembered where they were. He bounced toward the place where the girl had left them. When he had them in his hands, he bounced back to Ellen.

Ellen let out a cry as she saw the children begin to fight over Steve. The girl held Steve's legs in her hands. The boy held Steve's head in his hands. The two children began to pull. Steve let out a cry of pain.

Ellen hit the girl's leg with her chain. The child didn't seem to feel the blow. Ellen hit her again as hard as she could. The child let go of Steve's legs and looked down. Ellen bounced out of her way.

Then Don hit the boy with his chain. The boy let go of Steve. He began to fall through the air, his hands waving. Don and Ellen caught him as he fell.

"You OK?" Don asked him when he was on his feet again.

"So so," Steve answered when he had caught his breath. "But I'm not ready for another free fall. Why do those kids always pick on *me*?"

"Look out!" Ellen shouted.

Don and Steve looked up. The boy was reaching for them. They bounced along the ground with Ellen between them. As they ran, Don and Ellen dropped their heavy chains on the ground.

They were afraid to look back. They could hear the sounds of the giant boy as he ran after them. Every time the boy's feet hit the ground, it sounded like thunder.

Soon they came to a place where grass was growing. To them, the grass looked like young trees. They bounced into it and found themselves moving through what looked like a forest on Earth.

"Hold it!" Don shouted. "Stay still. Don't move. Get down on the ground. Maybe the boy won't be able to see us in this tall grass."

The three of them lay on the ground as the boy walked through the grass looking for them. The girl joined him, but she soon gave up looking. When she said something to the boy, both of them started back toward their houses.

"I think we're safe now," Don said. "They're leaving. So let's go." They got up and started toward the steps that led to the top of the planet.

Ellen looked back over her shoulder. "Estrada!" she said. "Chadrow, look!"

Steve and Don looked back. They saw a snake as big as a tunnel moving fast through the grass toward the children. Its open mouth was full of many sharp teeth.

"Come on, Drake," Don said. "We don't want that snake to see us!"

But Ellen stopped to watch the snake. It kept on moving fast toward the children, who hadn't seen it. Ellen shouted to them. She told them to run. But they didn't hear her.

Then she made up her mind. She went back

toward the children and the snake. Steve shouted at her to come back. But she didn't listen. She moved as fast as she could. Even though she didn't know what she was going to do, she felt that she had to do something. It was clear to her that the snake was out to kill them.

Running toward the children, Ellen shouted as loud as she could. The children heard her this time and looked down. As the girl began to pick Ellen up, she saw the snake. She screamed and started to run toward her house.

When the boy saw the snake, he backed away. His mouth was open, and yet he didn't make a sound.

The snake moved toward Ellen. It snapped at her. But she jumped to one side. Then the snake moved toward the boy.

Ellen looked around for something to use against the snake. She saw the chain that she had dropped a little while ago and picked it up. As she did, the snake caught the boy's leg. It circled his body and began to drag him down. The boy screamed.

Ellen went up close to the snake. She lifted her chain and began to swing it in a circle over her head. When the snake saw what she was doing, it tried to bite her. But its head couldn't reach Ellen because its body was wrapped around the boy.

Ellen hit at it with her chain. The chain cut right through the snake's body. Its head fell to the ground.

Still screaming, the boy got up and ran toward his house as Ellen rushed back to Steve and Don.

"Drake! You're sure full of surprises," shouted Steve as she ran up to them.

"I never know what you're going to do next," said Don.

"Maybe that's a good thing," Ellen said with a laugh. But she knew it had been a very close call.

They began to bounce along toward the steps that led above the ground. Behind them, the girl came out of the house and let out a cry. The boy came out, too, and they ran after their pets.

Ellen, Don, and Steve reached the steps. They began to run up them with the children behind. Just then a voice like thunder sounded. The children stopped in their tracks. Then they turned around and climbed back down the steps.

Out of breath, Steve asked, "What made them go back?"

"That was the girl's mother calling," Don said. "I'd guess that she didn't want the girl to follow us up and out into the sun. The sun would kill her if she did."

"Come on!" Ellen said. She began to run up the steps. But then, suddenly, she stopped. There were noises above them. Then came the sound of a human voice: "Keep at it, you dirty dogs. Don't stop now!"

"That's Captain Kane!" Ellen whispered. "He must be still trying to get that big jewel out of here."

"Listen to me," Steve whispered. "We've got to get out of here before Kane and his friends do. Now there's one thing I'm pretty sure of. I don't think he'll leave here without that jewel. So here's what we do."

He told them his plan. Then the three of them began to move up the steps. They didn't make a sound. Soon they caught sight of Captain Kane and his two crew members.

Carl and Tufo were rolling the heavy jewel up the steps. Captain Kane was in front of it. While his crew rolled the jewel up the steps, he shouted at them.

Don moved forward to come up behind the two crew members. He grabbed Tufo by the legs and threw him over his shoulder. The alien bounced down the steps. Then Don grabbed Carl and threw him back down the steps toward Ellen and Steve.

Steve grabbed Tufo and pushed him down the rest of the steps. At the same time, Ellen hit Carl, took his gun, and rolled him down the steps. Then she and Steve ran up the steps to join Don.

"Stay back!" Captain Kane shouted at them. He pointed his gun at them. "Drop that gun!" he ordered Ellen.

She dropped it. As she did so, Don grabbed a burning stick from one of the fires in the wall. He moved around the jewel up toward Captain Kane, holding the fire in front of Captain Kane's face.

To get away from the fire, Captain Kane began to circle around the jewel away from Don. When Kane got below the jewel on the steps, Don gave a shout.

"*Help me push!*" He put his shoulder against the jewel.

Ellen and Steve ran up to Don to help him push the jewel. It began to move.

Captain Kane started to run down the steps when he saw what they were trying to do. “No, don’t!” he said.

But they only pushed the jewel harder.

Captain Kane tried to get out of its way. But the jewel picked up speed and came at him fast. He screamed as it knocked him down and rolled right over him. Then it kept on rolling down the steps.

Ellen looked down at Captain Kane's body. It was almost flat because of the great weight of the jewel. "Is he . . . ?"

"Yes," Steve said, "he's dead."

"Come on," Don said. "Let's get out of here before we run into any more trouble."

The three of them began to climb the steps. Soon they came out into the hot Zandarian sun.

"Voyager is safe!" Ellen shouted when she saw the spaceship. As she climbed into the control room she said to the men, "I've never been so glad to see a spaceship in my life. Here's a kiss, Voyager."

"WHAT A PLEASANT HUMAN HABIT," said Voyager.

They shut the door after them. Ellen started the jets and they lifted off fast. Soon Voyager left Zandar, land of the giants, and flew through space toward Galaxy 5.